"My Grandmother Is a Singing Yaya"

by Karen Scourby D'Arc

pictures by Diane Palmisciano

Orchard Books ♪ New York

An Imprint of Scholastic Inc.

ALLEN S HILL

Text copyright © 2001 by Karen Scourby D'Arc
Illustrations copyright © 2001 by Diane Palmisciano

Library of Congress Cataloging-in-Publication Data

D'Arc, Karen Scourby.
My grandmother is a singing Yaya / by Karen Scourby D'Arc ;
illustrated by Diane Palmisciano.
   p. cm.
Summary: Lulu loves to hear her Greek grandmother sing when they are alone, but she is embarrassed by her grandmother's exuberance in public—until a special picnic at school.
ISBN 0-439-29309-X (alk. paper)
[1. Grandmothers—Fiction. 2. Greek Americans—Fiction. 3. Singing—Fiction.]
I. Palmisciano, Diane, ill. II. Title.
PZ7.D2414 My 2001 [E]—dc21 00-39944

10 9 8 7 6 5 4 3 2 1   01 02 03 04 05

Printed in Mexico 49

First edition, November 2001

Book design by Mina Greenstein
The text of this book is set in 14 point Cheltenham.
The illustrations are oil pastel.

Dedicated with love
To my mother, the *original* Singing Yaya, Stephanie Scourby D'Arc
To my niece, Katherine Rae Corwin, and
To the memory of my yaya, Katherine Sidereas Scourby

–K.S.D.

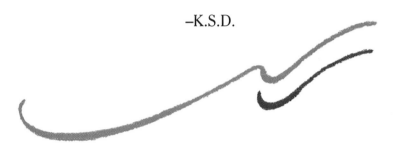

For Ana

–D.P.

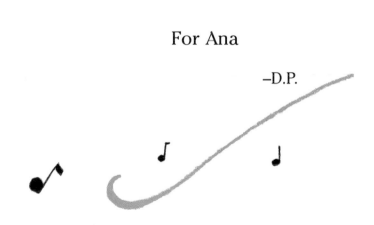

When I'm with my grandmother, I never know when she might burst into song. If we're walking down the street and pass a pet store, she'll open her mouth, take a deep breath, pause, and sing in her opera voice, "Dog, dog, what a darling dog!" or "Green and red is that feathered head!" She just sings about anything.

"Green and red is that feathered head!"

I look at the people passing by and try to tell them with my eyes, "She can't be stopped."
Yaya notices sometimes and shakes her head with a smile, saying, "I know, I know, I'm embarrassing you."

I call my grandmother "Yaya." That's Greek for grandma. Sometimes Yaya embarrasses me in front of my friends too.

"Nice hot soup for Juby joup," Yaya sang one day as she put a bowl of Yaya's Lemon Soup in front of my best friend. Juby never saw such a yellow soup before. I have to teach her about lots of Greek things.

"It's just the egg yolks, Juby. I know you'll like it if you try it."

"Lulu, do all yayas sing like that?" Juby asked me.

"I think it's just because Yaya was a singer on the stage," I said. I have to teach her about my grandmother too.

One time, when Yaya and I went to the movies, we saw a musical that she loved. Yaya clapped her hands at the end and shouted, "Bravo! Bravo! Bravo!" When the lights came up, everyone looked to

see who it was. By this time Yaya had started singing the movie's loudest song, and I had scrunched way down in my seat.

When we're alone, I like hearing Yaya sing. And I sing with her too. She sings all kinds of things. She teaches me folk songs from her mother's village in Greece. That's my great-Yaya, and I'm named after her. Yaya used to sing with her mother, and now she sings with me.

When she puts me to bed, Yaya rubs my back and sings a song about the sun, called "Eliamou." She says it soothes me. I say, "More, please, Yaya."

This week is the Grandparents' Day Picnic at school. I told my mother I wanted Yaya to come. "But, Mom," I said. "I want Yaya to act like the other grandmothers. That means no singing in the middle of everything."

Mom laughed. "If there is one thing Yaya does not do, it's act like everyone else."

On Grandparents' Day, I brought Yaya to the picnic. She had really been looking forward to it and sang the whole way:

"What a special day...,"
"We've packed a picnic"

basket full of goodies...,"

Welcome Grandparents

. . . and even a real song, "Oh, What a Beautiful Morning."

"Gee, Yaya. You must be tired of singing," I said with my fingers crossed as we arrived at school.

"Oh, Lulu, this is such fun," is all Yaya said.

I quickly looked around and found Juby. "How am I going to keep Yaya from singing in front of everybody?" I was worried.

"Can't you just ask her not to?" I guess Juby thought this was simple. She still had more to learn about Yaya.

"You don't understand, Juby. Yaya sings because, to her, everything is so much fun. I'll hurt her feelings if I ask her not to."

Yaya wanted us to do the gunnysack race. She said she was always good at that. "Hop, hop, hop," she said gaily as we started. Uh-oh. She could probably even sing while hopping. Sure enough, she opened her mouth, took a deep breath, and—

"Keep hopping, Yaya," I cried. "We might win." We made five hyper hops and came in second!

The teacher gave us a bouquet of balloons. Yaya was delighted. She opened her mouth, took a deep breath, and—

I grabbed her by the hand. "Come on,
Yaya, let's find a good spot."

I tried to pull her way over to the
far side of the lawn, but halfway there
she put the picnic basket down.

"No, Yaya, not here." But Yaya didn't pay attention. She spread her blanket and sat down, looking very happy with her place in the middle of the picnic.

Yaya always says that the
only thing she likes more
than singing is feeding her
grandchildren. She threw
open the basket and whipped
out Greek foods I love:

feta cheese,

stuffed grape leaves,

and *keftethes,* which are
meatballs.

I almost burst into song myself,

until I saw Yaya admiring the feast,
opening her mouth, taking a deep breath
again, and—

"Yaya, did you bring dessert?" She fished around in the picnic basket and pulled out baklava, my favorite. "Thanks for remembering, Yaya," I said.

Yaya gave me a hug. For just a moment, I let her hold me in her lap. I felt her take a deep breath, but this time I couldn't stop her.

"Oh, my Lulu," she sang out.

"How I love my Lulaki!"

I jumped out of her lap. "Yaya! No! Shh!" It was too late. Everyone was looking at us . . . and smiling.

ALLEN S HILL

The principal stood up. "Grandparents, I'd like you to help celebrate the school's fiftieth year by joining us in singing 'Happy Birthday.'" Then—I couldn't believe it—he turned and looked at Yaya and me. "And I'd like Lulu's grandmother to lead."

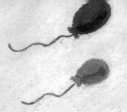

Yaya opened her mouth, took a deep breath, and launched into "Happy Birthday" with all her might. We all joined in. On the last note, Yaya's voice went way up high above the others. Everyone clapped.

I squeezed Yaya's hand. She smiled. Then we both took a bow in front of my whole school.

Now when Yaya and I walk down the street and she just sings about anything, I still look at the people passing by and tell them with my eyes, "She can't be stopped!" But sometimes, for the fun of it, I burst out singing, "MY GRANDMOTHER IS A SINGING YAYA!"